A Note to Parents and Caregivers:

Read-it! Joke Books are for children who are moving ahead on the amazing road to reading. These fun books support the acquisition and extension of reading skills as well as a love of books.

Published by the same company that produces *Read-it!* Readers, these books introduce the question/answer pattern that helps children expand their thinking about language structure and book formats.

When sharing a book with your child, read in short stretches, pausing often to talk about the pictures and the meaning of the book. The question/answer format works well for this purpose and provides an opportunity to talk about the language and meaning of the jokes. Have your child turn the pages and point to the pictures and familiar words. Read the story in a natural voice; have fun creating the voices of characters or emphasizing some important words. And be sure to reread favorite parts.

There is no right or wrong way to share books with children. Find time to read with your child, and pass on the legacy of literacy.

Adria F. Klein, Ph.D.
Professor Emeritus
California State University
San Bernardino, California

Managing Editor: Bob Temple
Creative Director: Terri Foley
Editors: Brenda Haugen, Nadia Higgins
Designers: John Moldstad, Amy Bailey
Page production: Picture Window Books
The illustrations in this book were prepared digitally.

Picture Window Books
5115 Excelsior Boulevard
Suite 232
Minneapolis, MN 55416
1-877-845-8392
www.picturewindowbooks.com

Printed in the United States of America.

Library of Congress Cataloging-in-Publication Data
Dahl, Michael.
Open up and laugh! : a book of knock-knock jokes / written by Michael Dahl;
illustrated by Brian Jensen.
p. cm. — (Read-it! joke books)
ISBN 1-4048-0237-1
1. Knock-knock jokes. I. Jensen, Brian, ill. II. Title.
PN6231.K55D435 2003
818'.602—dc21
                                                                    2003004801

Open Up
And Laugh!

A Book of Knock-Knock Jokes

Michael Dahl • Illustrated by Brian Jensen

Reading Advisers:
Adria F. Klein, Ph.D.
Professor Emeritus, California State University
San Bernardino, California

Susan Kesselring, M.A., Literacy Educator
Rosemount-Apple Valley-Eagan (Minnesota) School District

PICTURE WINDOW BOOKS
Minneapolis, Minnesota

Knock knock.
Who's there?
Little old lady.
Little old lady who?

I didn't know you could yodel!

Knock knock.
Who's there?
Dakota.
Dakota who?

Dakota's too big for me.
May I borrow yours?

Knock knock.
Who's there?
Snow.
Snow who?

Snowbody here but me! 7

Knock knock.
Who's there?
Water.
Water who?

8   Water you doing in my house?

Knock knock.
   Who's there?
Wooden shoe.
   Wooden shoe who?

Wooden shoe like to know?

Knock knock.
    Who's there?
Adam.
    Adam who?

	1	2	3	4	5	6	7	8	9
Home	1	0	0	1	4	0	3		
Visitor	0	0	3	2	2	1	0		

Adam up, and
tell me the score.

11

Knock knock.
    Who's there?
Radio.
    Radio who?

12   Radio not, here I come.

Knock knock.
Who's there?
Statue.
Statue who?

Statue making all
that noise in there? 13

Knock knock.
Who's there?
Avenue.
Avenue who?

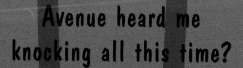

Avenue heard me
knocking all this time?

Knock knock.
  Who's there?
Dozen.
  Dozen who?

Eggs

Dozen anybody ever
answer the door?

Knock knock.
    Who's there?
Tish.
    Tish who?

That's good for blowing your nose! 17

Knock knock.
Who's there?
Wah.
Wah who?

Well, you don't have
to get so excited about it!

Knock knock.
Who's there?
Roach.
Roach who?

Roach you a letter,
but you never wrote back.

19

Knock knock.
        Who's there?
Pasture.
        Pasture who?

Pasture bedtime, isn't it?

Knock knock.
  Who's there?
Tuba.
  Tuba who?

Tuba Toothpaste.

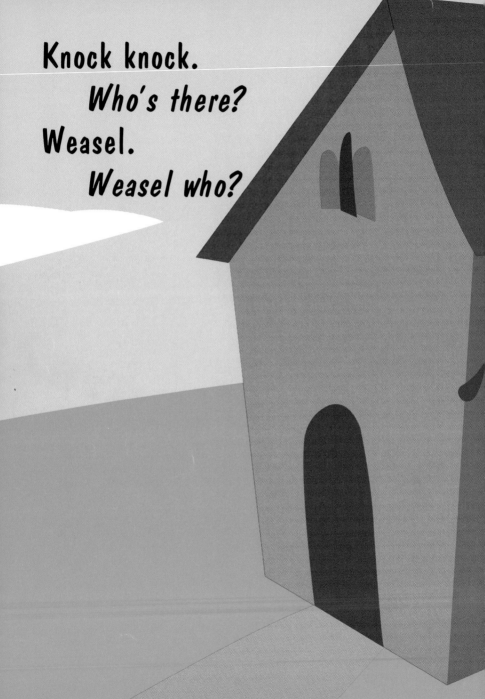

Knock knock.
Who's there?
Weasel.
Weasel who?

Weasel while you work!

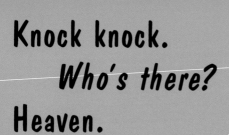

Knock knock.
  Who's there?
Heaven.
  Heaven who?

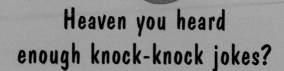

Heaven you heard
enough knock-knock jokes?

24